Spotlight on Stacey

You are now entering 1750

written and illustrated by
Maryann Cocca-Leffler

Kane Press, Inc.
New York

To the children of Colonial Amherst, NH—Maryann Cocca-Leffler

Acknowledgements: Our thanks to Martha Noblick, Librarian, Historic Deerfield, for helping us make this book as accurate as possible.

Library of Congress Cataloging-in-Publication Data

Cocca-Leffler, Maryann, 1958-
   Spotlight on Stacey / written and illustrated by Maryann Cocca-Leffler.
     p. cm. —- (Social studies connects)
   Summary: When Stacey's class has to perform in a play about colonial America, preparation and the surprise appearance of a sheep onstage help her overcome her chronic stage fright.
   ISBN-13: 978-1-57565-236-8 (alk. paper)
   ISBN-10: 1-57565-236-6 (alk. paper)
   [1. Theater—Fiction. 2. Schools—Fiction. 3. Stage fright—Fiction.
  4. United States—History—Colonial period, ca. 1600-1775—Fiction.]
  I. Title.
  PZ7.C638Sp 2007
  [E]—dc22
                          2006026407

10 9 8 7 6 5 4 3 2 1

First published in the United States of America in 2007 by Kane Press, Inc.
Printed in Hong Kong.

Social Studies Connects is a registered trademark of Kane Press, Inc.

Book Design: Edward Miller

www.kanepress.com

"Class, we're going on a trip!" said Ms. Diaz.

"Where are we going?" everyone asked at once.

"Back in time—to 1750," Ms. Diaz told us. "You'll soon be colonists in a new land."

"Can't we just go to Super Funland?" Eric joked.

"Who needs wild rides when we have a new world to build?" said Ms. Diaz.

A new world, I thought. Very cool!

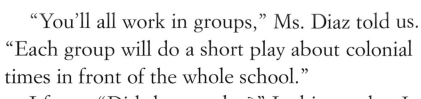

"You'll all work in groups," Ms. Diaz told us. "Each group will do a short play about colonial times in front of the whole school."

I froze. "Did she say play?" I whispered to Lee.

"Yes," said Lee.

"Did she say, in front of the whole school?" I asked.

Lee nodded. "Don't worry, Stacey. It'll be okay."

Farm Family, 1750 Stacey— Daughter (Age 10)

A **colony** is a settlement that is ruled by another country. The 13 American colonies were ruled by England.

I was glad Lee was in my group. She was my best friend and knew all about my terrible stage fright. Lee loved the spotlight. I'd rather eat dirt than talk in front of a crowd of people.

"Okay, group," Eric said in a deep voice. "We're a colonial farm family. And I am the father. I rule!"

We looked at our project sheets. Lee was the mother, Mara was the grandmother, and I was the ten-year-old girl. She'll be a girl who doesn't talk, I thought.

1492	1607	1620	1732	1776
Columbus lands in the New World	First permanent colony: Jamestown, VA	Pilgrims land at Plymouth Rock, MA	George Washington born in VA	U.S.A. created, colonies become states

When I got home, I told Mom about the project.
"Stacey, it's going to be fine," she assured me.

"Fine?" I said. "Remember the camp play? I
forgot my lines and ran offstage—and Mr. Davis
had to play Goldilocks for the rest of the show."

"I'll call your Aunt Kiki," said Mom. "After all,
she *is* an actress. Maybe she can help."

"I need all the help I can get," I said.

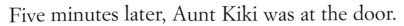

Five minutes later, Aunt Kiki was at the door.

"This is so exciting!" she said, rushing into the house. "Another actress in the family!"

She plopped a cap on my head. "I borrowed this from the costume department!"

"But—"

Colonial girls and women almost always kept their heads covered—with hats, hoods, or caps like the one Stacey is wearing. It was the fashion—and they didn't need to wash their hair as often!

7

"You have to LIVE the part!"
said Aunt Kiki. "Remember when
I got hired for that fried chicken
commercial? I BECAME a chicken!"
"How could I forget?" I said.
For weeks my Aunt Kiki had
clucked around in a chicken suit.
"I studied those chickens at
Mabel's farm night and day,"
she went on. "Research
is important."

"But what about my stage fright?" I asked.

"Stacey, if you get to know your character, you'll forget all about it," Aunt Kiki told me.

"But how can I get to know the colonists? I can't go back in time!"

"Yes, you can!" said Aunt Kiki. "Be ready at seven tomorrow morning. We have research to do!"

Colonists were people who left their country to settle, or make homes, in a new land.

Many settlers came to the New World from Spain, France, Sweden, and Holland. But most came from England.

Some people came so they could be free to follow their own religion. Some came to make better lives. And some came just for the adventure!

At seven sharp, we were on the road. Two hours later I felt like I *was* back in time.

A man dressed in a wig and funny pants bowed to us. "Good day," he said. "Welcome to Colonial Village."

"Why is he acting like that?" I whispered.

"All the people here speak and act as if they're really in the 1750s," said Aunt Kiki.

It was like a time warp.

Aunt Kiki pointed to a sign. "Wigs for sale! Let's go in."

WIGS

Before I knew it, Aunt Kiki was modeling the latest 1750 style. It looked like a woman's wig, but it was for a man!

"What's this for?" she asked the wigmaker.

"That is a powder-puffing tool to keep the wigs white," the lady said, "but touch not—"

"Oops!" It was too late.

Wigs were very popular in the 1700s for rich men and sometimes women. They were made of human or horse hair. Some wigs cost as much as a whole outfit!

11

A New England Village
1750

TRAVELING
Some colonists had horses, but most people walked everywhere. So they didn't go far from home!

The MEETINGHOUSE was both a church and a place for town meetings.

VILLAGE GREEN
Townspeople could let their farm animals graze here.

We coughed our way out of the shop and onto a village green. Everyone was busy. I saw a blacksmith, a woman making candles, and a man chopping wood. Even the kids were working.

CRAFTSPEOPLE made and fixed things colonists needed. The cooper made barrels. The wheelwright made wheels. The cobbler made shoes.

The TAVERN was part hotel, part restaurant.

The TOWN CRIER was like a human newspaper. He shouted out the news.

GRAVEYARD
Many colonists died young of sicknesses we can cure today.

A person who broke the law could be locked up in STOCKS.

BLACKSMITHS made and mended horseshoes, metal tools, locks, even muskets.

13

I saw a girl my age sitting at a spinning wheel.

"What are you doing?" I asked.

"I am spinning this wool into yarn," she said in an English accent. "I will weave the yarn into cloth and sew myself a skirt."

"Why don't you just go to the mall?" I said.

"What is a mall?" the girl asked.

"She really *is* behind the times," I whispered to Aunt Kiki.

"Stacey, this is Beth," Aunt Kiki said. "She played the witch in my last show. You probably don't recognize her without her green makeup. Beth is acting the role of a farmer's daughter— just like your part at school. She'll help you *think* like a colonist."

Beth smiled. "It would be wise to change your garment. We have many chores to do."

"I signed up to work for the blacksmith," said Aunt Kiki. "You girls have fun!"

Many colonists spoke with English accents because they came from England.

shearing

carding (untangling)

spinning

dyeing

weaving

sewing

Colonists had no electricity. After sunset, they had to see by the light of candles and oil lamps—or go to bed early!

Almost every colonial family had a Bible.

There were no right and left shoes in colonial times. Shoes were all the same.

The colonists did not have running water in their houses. They brought in water from a well. Toilets were outside in little sheds called "outhouses."

Sparks from the fireplace could set a whole house ablaze. A bucket of water was like a colonial fire extinguisher.

Pans had very long handles so cooks could stand away from the flames.

I followed Beth into her tiny farmhouse. "How many people live here?"

"My parents, two brothers, and grandmother," answered Beth.

Wow! How do they all fit? I wondered.

I quickly changed into a heavy skirt, a cap, and strange-looking leather shoes. The shoes felt funny.

Colonists did laundry in a wooden tub—with washboards and homemade soap. Sometimes they used the laundry tub for baths, too.

All morning I worked with Beth—
and I mean *worked!*

We spun more wool,

Why are they
called hornbooks?

Because they are
made of cow horn!

studied verses from
our hornbooks,

and picked wildflowers
to make dye for
Beth's skirt.

Hornbooks held one piece of paper
with the alphabet or prayers on it.
A see-through sheet of cow horn kept
the paper clean. Paper cost a lot!

Finally I sat down. But not for long!

"Stacey, I shall make soup now," said Beth. "And there is butter to be churned."

I churned away while Beth cut up vegetables and added them to a simmering pot. They sure could use a microwave around here!

Colonial girls stayed busy. They made candles and soap, knitted and sewed, cared for farm animals, cleaned, and made meals. Colonial boys hunted, farmed, and learned job skills. On top of all that, many kids went to school six days a week—yes, even on Saturdays!

Soon it was time to leave 1750 behind. Aunt Kiki met me at the farmhouse. I laughed when I saw her.

"Shoeing horses is a messy job!" she told me.

Just then Beth came out of the house. She looked so different! "Feels good to be in jeans," she said.

"Sure does," I said. "Hey! Where's your accent?"

"Gone—just like the costume!" Beth grinned. "Now it's back to the 21st century!"

On Monday I told my group all about visiting Colonial Village. We wrote our play in no time.

But when I started to practice lines, my stomach did a backflip. "I can't do this," I moaned.

"I shall take pity on you, daughter," said Eric. "You may spin wool onstage while I give your speech."

"Thank you, Father," I said. *Whew!*

My new job was to work on props and costumes. Aunt Kiki was happy to help us do research.

After school she taught us how to make cornhusk dolls. Eric's doll looked more like a ghost.

She showed us some colonial games and read to us about colonial manners. Boy, they had a lot of rules!

Bow or curtsy before you speak. Spit not in the fire. Do not blow your nose with the hand that takes the meat.

Boo.

When he was growing up, George Washington copied more than a hundred rules from a book of manners—like the one Aunt Kiki is reading. He was very polite!

Our set for the play was the inside of a colonial farmhouse. We made it out of cardboard and paint. It looked awesome!

Finally we were ready for the show.

Colonial children played with dolls, tops, marbles, cards, kites, jump ropes, and puzzles—just like kids do today! But back then most toys were homemade.

On Friday the auditorium was buzzing. I went onstage and nervously took my place. Then I felt a nudge on my leg.

Baaa. I looked down. It was a sheep. A real sheep! Aunt Kiki peeked around the curtain. "I thought he would be a great prop!" she said.

"We can't—" I started to say.

But it was too late.

The curtained opened. The audience gasped.
All eyes were on the sheep.

"I am Mary Eaton," began Lee. "This is . . .
Achoo! This is my husband, John. *Achoo!* . . . and
my . . . *Achoo!* . . ."

Oh, no! Lee must be allergic to the sheep. She
*achoo*ed herself right off the stage.

Quickly, Mara stepped forward. "I am Grandma Eaton. This is my famous peach preserve. We need to store food for our long, cold winters. We spend many hours preserving and drying our—"

The colonists had lots of ways to keep food from going bad—like pickling, smoking, drying, and salting. They made "soup in your pocket"—dried meat you could carry around until you wanted to add water and eat it!

Just then the sheep got into the pot of peaches.
Eric tried to shoo him offstage, but the sheep
got hold of Mara's apron and began chasing her.
Peaches were flying everywhere.
Our play was turning into one big disaster!

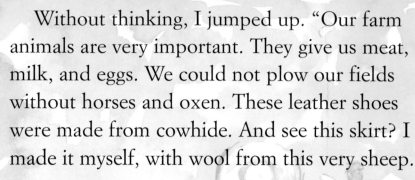

Without thinking, I jumped up. "Our farm animals are very important. They give us meat, milk, and eggs. We could not plow our fields without horses and oxen. These leather shoes were made from cowhide. And see this skirt? I made it myself, with wool from this very sheep.

Sheep were so important, there were laws about them. In some places, sheep under two years old could not be sold for food. Anyone who harmed a sheep would find himself in big trouble!

"Life on our farm is not easy. We work hard. But we work together. Everyone helps—even the sheep."

The audience clapped and cheered. I heard
Aunt Kiki yell, "That's my niece—the actress!"
   I could hardly believe it. The play was over—
and I'd survived.

Lee came out from backstage as our group stepped forward. "*Achoo!* Stacey, you saved the play!" she said. "*Achoo!* And your stage fright— it's cured!"

"What stage fright?" I said. And we took one last bow.

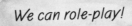

We can role-play!

MAKING CONNECTIONS

There's only one way for you to visit 1750. No, it's not with a time machine. It's by role-playing! That means using your imagination to pretend you're someone else and maybe someplace else. Stacey and Beth pretend to be colonial girls. Who would you like to be?

Look Back
- Look at pages 10–14. What roles are the actors at Colonial Village playing?
- What is Stacey doing on pages 16–17? How does it help her play the role of a girl from 1750?
- Read pages 28–29. How did Stacey's role-playing at Colonial Village help her get over her stage fright?

Try This!
Role-playing is a great way to connect to the past. Form a group with friends or classmates and create your own play! Give a different role to each person in the group. What role would you like to play? Blacksmith? Town crier? The sheep? Maybe you'd rather be a cowhand in the Wild West—or the first astronaut to walk on the moon! Pick any place or time that interests you.

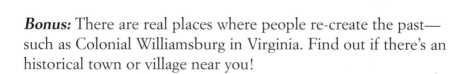

Bonus: There are real places where people re-create the past—such as Colonial Williamsburg in Virginia. Find out if there's an historical town or village near you!